"Will this storm ever end?" Maribel said as she watched the snow collect in the corners of the glass panes. A particularly large flake glued itself to the window. It reminded her of a star. It was then that she also noticed a mound of snow piling high on her front stoop. "If it gets any deeper, we may not be able to open the door."

The Unicorn Tales series

Amie Borst

illustrated by Roch Hercka

Summary: When Callie's magic breaks and a flood
threatens their kingdom, Maribel must find the strength to
save them both.
BISAC: JUVENILE FICTION/Animals/Dragons,
Unicorns & Mythical. JUVENILE
FICTION/Readers/Chapter books. JUVENILE
FICTION/Social Themes/Self Esteem & Self Reliance.
JUVENILE FICION/Fantasy & Magic.
For more information about this title, write us at Mystery
Goose Press P.O. Box 86627 Vint Hill, VA 20187

Printed in the United States of America.
Library of Congress Control Number: 2021914355
ISBN: 978-1-948882-23 -1 (paperback)
ISBN: 978-1-948882-22 -4 (ebook)

ISLE
OF
AVONLEA

THREE FRIENDS
STREAM

NORTH LAK

HOLLYBERRY GARDE

DREAMSICLE POND

DRAGON SEA

DRAGONFIRE
FOREST

KINGDOM
OF
AUTUMNSEVE

BRAVERY
BRIDGE

STREAM OF KINDNESS

PURPLE
PUMPKIN PATCH

TROLL THICKET

SUM

COLORFUL
CLOVER PATCH

SOUTH
LAKE

MOUN

MERPEOPLE
ISLAND

BROWNIE BOG

S

Kingdom of Wintersend

Kingdom of Wintersend, how we love thee.
Kingdom of Wintersend, oh how lovely.
Friends are kind and friends are winsome,
Always in the Wintersend Kingdom.

Chapter 1

*M*aribel looked out the window of her cottage and sighed as snow came down in sheets of white. It had been snowing heavily for several days in the Kingdom of Wintersend and there was no end in sight.

While Maribel normally enjoyed the fresh powder that Callie created, this was a bit much. In some areas of her kingdom, the snow had become knee-deep, making it difficult to travel. Over the last few hours, the snowfall had become terribly dense. When Maribel did go outside, she couldn't see beyond her nose. In fact, she'd never seen a storm like this. Not in all her days of living in the Kingdom of Wintersend on the beautiful Isle of Avonlea.

Wintersend had become a cold and worrisome winter land.

"Will this storm ever end?" Maribel said as she watched the snow collect in the corners of the glass panes. A particularly large flake glued itself to the window. It reminded her of a star. It was then that she also noticed a mound of snow piling high on her front stoop. "If it gets any deeper, we may not be able to open the door."

"Or the windows," a pegacorn named Heidi said, pointing a hoof toward the gathering snow. Heidi was one of Maribel's friends. The pair had met earlier that morning for a steaming mug of pink hollyberry cocoa. The two friends often went skating on Dreamsicle Pond together. Sometimes they would race to the top of Mount Wintersend and slide down the Three Friend's Stream. But not today. Or anytime soon. The blizzard kept them inside. "What would we do then?"

"We could be stuck inside forever." Maribel's concern grew by the minute. She spread her white wings wide and flapped them, stirring quite a blast of air. Her icy blue mane swayed, and strands of hair fell against the side of her face.

"I certainly hope not." Heidi shivered and turned away from the gust. She then stretched her own wings. Her beautiful coat of white sparkled and glistened just like the snowflakes. If it weren't for her mane and tail which were a shade of apricot, she'd blend in perfectly with the freshly fallen snow. Heidi's horn, a twist of orange and white, reminded Maribel of creamsicle sorbet. "There's just so much snow!"

"This is terrible." Maribel's stomach felt a bit queasy. She dreaded the idea of an endless blizzard.

"And just think," Heidi said, her breath fogging up the window so there was nothing but a gray pane between her and the outside world. "It wasn't long ago when winter threatened to end forever."

"I almost wish it would!" Maribel had begun to tire of the storm. But now she worried. "This is a troublesome amount of snow."

"Agreed." Heidi's warm breath left another mark on the cold window. Her tail twitched and Heidi jumped. "Stop that," she whispered to her tail.

Maribel shook her head. "What can we do?"

"Nothing," Heidi chuffed. "I'm not sure

there's anything to be done." Her tail twitched again, and Heidi squinted.

"Maybe I should see if Callie needs any help," Maribel said. "It's unlike her to make this much snow."

"That's not a bad idea," Heidi said as her tail twitched a third time. "I'll just get my cloak and we can be on our way." She turned to grab her special white cape, which was trimmed with shiny, silver threads.

Suddenly, the front door burst open and with it came a flurry of bitter, cold snowflakes. A figure stood in the doorway.

Maribel gasped. "What are you doing here?"

"It's so cold outside and the snow is so deep." Heidi removed the cape from the hook. She carried it between her teeth and trotted toward the figure.

"You must have had a long, and dangerous journey," Maribel exclaimed. "Come inside and rest a bit. We'll bring you some pink holly-berry cocoa."

"There's no time for cocoa!" the figure said, stepping inside the cottage. King Holly-

berry straightened his back, and it let out a
loud crack.

Maribel looked at Heidi in shock. King
Hollyberry never left his throne on top of Mount
Wintersend. To see him here was simply unheard
of. "You must warm up by the fire for a bit then."
Maribel trotted over to the king and nudged him.

"What's wrong?" Heidi mumbled with the
cape still between her teeth as she tipped her
head toward the king.

"She's sick!" King Hollyberry announced with a clang of his staff. He brushed a thick layer of freshly fallen snow from his coat. Then he removed his crown and shook it off before returning it to his head.

"Who's sick?" Maribel gave the king another nudge.

"Callie!" the king exclaimed. "The Pegacorn of Winter. Who else would I be talking about?" A puddle of melted snow began to gather at his feet. He stepped over it and approached the fire, resting his staff against the mantel.

The cloak fell from Heidi's mouth as she stared with her jaw agape. "This is worse than I thought!"

"Oh, it's much worse," the king said as he stood in front of the dancing flames, warming his hands. "You haven't yet heard the biggest news of all."

Chapter 2

"There's more?" Heidi asked.

"Much more!" The king clapped his hands together.

"Tell us," Maribel said as she flicked her tail, feeling a wee bit impatient.

King Hollyberry took a deep breath, his chest puffing out before he released the air in one big woosh. "Callie's magic is broken."

Maribel's mouth dropped open. "So that's why the snow hasn't stopped."

"That *is* terrible," Heidi said as she pinned her ears back. "We should help her!"

Maribel flapped her wings, her front hooves lifting slightly off the ground, as she neighed loudly. "What can be done?"

"I was hoping the two of you might have an idea." The king looked at the pegacorns, his gaze falling first on Maribel and then on Heidi.

"I hadn't thought about what we could do,"

7

Heidi said shaking her head. "Maybe that was the first thing I should have done."

"That makes two of us," Maribel said to Heidi. Then she turned to the king. "But how did you come to learn this?"

King Hollyberry exhaled. "It's something that's been handed down to me. When a unicorn becomes sick, their magic breaks."

"I had no idea," Heidi said with a whinny. "What will become of things?"

"This is just the beginning." King Hollyberry wrung his hands and grumbled, "Or possibly the end."

"Of what?" Maribel asked.

"Avonlea!' The worried king picked up his staff and began to pace back and forth. He stroked his beard with one hand, while he carried the staff in the other, keeping it tucked behind his back. The train of his robe dragged behind him on the wood floor. "When a unicorn's magic breaks, it can throw off the balance of the entire island!"

"Oh, no!" Maribel cried. "We can't allow that to happen to Avonlea."

"Precisely." The king paused, clasping his hands on the staff behind his back. "That's why when I saw it was still snowing after all this time, I decided to pay her a visit."

"We were just heading there ourselves," Heidi said.

"Yes, yes. A most excellent idea," King Hollyberry mumbled to himself as he continued to pace the floor. "We must find a way to help her, and we must do so quickly."

Maribel gazed out the window at the snow gathering outside her door. She wanted to help Callie. She wanted the snow to stop. But she disliked the idea of going out into a blizzard. Maribel began to long for a visit to any of the three other kingdoms on Avonlea, but especially the Kingdom of Summerstart where sunshine warmed the land every day. "But the snow's so deep."

King Hollyberry marched over to the window and placed his hands on the cold glass, the staff clanging against the pane. "Too much snow!"

"How can Callie make snow if she's sick and her magic is broken?" Maribel asked. Usually when the snow fell, Callie was soaring high above the mountains. But she'd also been known to make snow whenever and wherever she wished.

"Callie can make snow from her hooves, she can make it from her horn, or she can command it from the clouds," the king said, smoothing his long white beard. "A unicorn's magic can work even when she's sick. In fact, sometimes that's when it gets out of control. That's precisely why it's broken!"

Heidi stepped toward the king. "If we can get her better, then her magic will be mended?"

"Indeed!" The king banged his staff on the ground, and it made a loud crack. "But if we don't hurry, soon the entire kingdom will be buried."

"That would be a disaster," Heidi said. "What would happen to the other kingdoms of Avonlea?"

Maribel turned sharply. "What would happen to *us*?"

"As long as the pegacorns of Wintersend can fly to the top of the mountain, they'll be safe," Heidi said. Her tail twitched and she gave it a sharp look.

"She's right. It's the unicorns in the other kingdoms that could be harmed. Their crops could all be destroyed, too." King Hollyberry clasped his hands around his staff and tapped it against the wood floor.

"Not the purple pumpkins!" Maribel cried. "Or the colorful clover and sparkle fruit."

King Hollyberry groaned. "That's why we need to put a stop to it."

"But how can we do that?" Heidi swished her long tail. It swung back and forth like a pendulum.

Maribel paced in front of the window. As she took one step after another, she thought of things that could help. Pumpkins and hollyberries always made her feel better. Maybe it would help Callie, too. But would it be enough? "I think I know how we can help!"

"You do?" The king's forehead wrinkled as he opened his eyes wide.

"I believe so," Maribel said with a nod. "It's worth a try. I'll go visit her right now."

"What will you say?" Heidi asked.

"I'm not going to *say* anything. I'm going to *do* something." Maribel chuffed as she shook her powdery blue mane. "I'll bring her some warm purple pumpkin soup and sparkling pink hollyberry cocoa."

"Can I help?" Heidi trotted alongside Maribel.

"Would you mind making the purple pumpkin soup?" Maribel asked. "Yours is the best in the kingdom."

"Why thank you!" Heidi blushed. "I'd be happy to." She smiled at Maribel. "I seem to recall that your sparkle fruit tart is the tastiest on all of Wintersend."

Maribel gasped. "That's an excellent idea!"

"What?" Heidi asked.

"A sparkle fruit tart! Callie would enjoy that, too." Maribel reared up with excitement, flapping her large, white wings. A gust of wind blew through the room.

Heidi took a step back, turning her face from the breeze. "But we don't have any sparkle fruit left."

"Then perhaps I need to make a quick trip to the Kingdom of Springsmorn." Maribel pranced toward the door.

"These are brilliant and thoughtful ideas," King Hollyberry said. "But I'm not sure it's enough."

Maribel whinnied. "Why not?"

"She needs medicine," the king said, his eyes lighting up. "That's it!"

"What is?" Maribel tipped her head, studying the king.

King Hollyberry wrung his hands as he began to pace the floor again. A wood board creaked beneath his feet as he stopped suddenly and exclaimed, "The medicine! I remember a special flower said to cure all unicorns and pegacorns of any ailment."

"You do?" Maribel reared up, neighing loudly as she flapped her wings.

"What's it called?" Heidi asked.

"If memory serves correctly, it's something about a meadow," King Hollyberry said. "Why yes, that's it. Meadowsweet!"

"Excellent!" Maribel tapped her hooves on the floor. "Where can we find it?"

King Hollyberry pulled a small leather-bound book out of the sleeve of his robe. "It says here…"—he flipped through the worn pages, running his finger over the words— "that it can be located on the banks of the Three Friends Stream where it joins with North Lake."

"But that's a terrible journey in this blizzard." Heidi furrowed her brow. "Traveling that far north in Wintersend would be extremely difficult."

"And dangerous," the king added.

Maribel planted her hooves and lifted her chin in the air. "It's a risk I'm willing to take."

ing Hollyberry glanced sideways at Maribel. "It's much too treacherous in this storm."

"Is there another choice?" Maribel asked. It wasn't really a question. She knew it needed to be done.

The king pursed his lips and nodded. "You've made an excellent point. Someone must go and do this if we're to help Callie. It's the only way to save the kingdom. Perhaps even the entire Isle of Avonlea."

"Then I will do it," Maribel said as she clopped her front hooves on the floor.

"Should I go with you?" Heidi asked. "A journey is always better with company."

"No, you stay and make the soup." Maribel flapped her wings. "I'll meet you at Callie's house in a jiffy."

"Are you sure?" King Hollyberry asked as the door suddenly blew open.

Maribel gasped and stumbled backward as snow poured in through the opening. She shivered, quickly regained her footing, and pushed the door closed. "I'm absolutely certain. But first, please tell me what the flower looks like, so I know what to search for." Maribel peeked over the crook of the king's elbow as he cradled the book in his hands.

The king pointed to the image of the Meadowsweet flower. "This is it right here."

"It's beautiful!" Maribel exclaimed. The flower was like nothing Maribel had ever seen before. Meadowsweet had multiple tiny, white star-shaped blossoms on a single stem.

"It is indeed," the king said. "But you must be careful with it."

Heidi peered into the pages of the book. "Is it fragile?"

"No, no. Nothing like that." King Hollyberry shook his head.

"Then what is it?" Maribel asked.

The king drew in a long breath. "The flower has been known to cause a deep sleep."

"That could be dangerous," Heidi nickered.

"That's precisely my concern." King Hollyberry traced his finger on the page, outlining the shape of the flower. "Bring back just one stem but be sure to keep it away from your nose. It'll tempt you with its fragrance, so you must remain watchful and not breathe it in."

"I can do that," Maribel said. "Tell me, how could it survive in all this snow?"

The king huffed then laughed, holding his belly. "That's the magic of this flower. It's what makes it so powerful."

"I see. Then I will be extra careful," Maribel said.

"Then it is done," King Hollyberry said. "You'll make the journey to the Three Friends Stream, and we'll prepare the food. We will meet you at Callie's house."

"Let me offer my cloak." Heidi trotted off toward the door where she had dropped her cape earlier. She returned with it a moment later, carrying it between her teeth.

"Most excellent idea. It'll keep you warm," King Hollyberry said as he draped the cloth over Maribel's back. He then fastened the ties around her neck.

"Thank you." Maribel nodded. Then, with a chuff, said, "I'll see you soon, my friends. Please send Callie my well wishes."

"Be safe, Maribel!" Heidi flicked her apricot tail which had a pretty hue to it in the light of the fire. She pinned her ears and lowered her head.

The king opened the door. "Return with care," he said as he patted the pegacorn's withers.

"You can count on me." Maribel stepped out into the cold, leaving the warmth of her home behind her. She smiled at Heidi and the king who waved from the front window. Then she turned toward the bleak storm, which fell in thick blankets of white.

Maribel squinted, struggling to see ahead. "The snowfall is much too heavy to fly. I can't even tell which direction I need to go. My only choice is to walk."

Still, Maribel believed she could do this. All she needed was to find her way to the Three Friends Stream and locate the Meadowsweet flower. Its healing properties were the only hope she had of saving her friend and the Kingdom of Wintersend.

Maribel kept her head down, the cape flapping behind her as she dodged the storm. She trudged through the village making her way to the great mountain in the north. She pushed onward, feeling frustrated she couldn't see beyond the thickness of the storm.

With each step, the thick and dense snow grew deeper and deeper until it passed her knees. Soon she would be buried beneath a mountain of snow, and then she'd never be able to help anyone.

"There has to be a better way," Maribel said, shaking snow from her beautiful coat of white. Her mane froze in thick clumps of icy blue and it slapped against her face with a sharp smack. "Ouch!" She reared up, flapping her wings, and created a powerful breeze which pushed the free-falling snowflakes away. A path cut through the storm, clearing way for Maribel.

"That's more like it!" Maribel quickly trotted ahead, beating her feathered wings. The light snowflakes of the storm blew away. "That's it! If my wings can send gusts of wind to push the flakes, the same should happen when I fly! Then I'll get there much faster!" Maribel whinnied. "But I have an even better idea. If I can get *above* the storm, I should be able to see everything below. Then I'll have a clear path straight to Three Friends Stream."

Soon she took flight, soaring high above the clouds.

But there was another problem ahead.

One Maribel never saw coming.

"*H*eavens to Avonlea!" Maribel said, spinning in a circle. The world below her was completely hidden by thick, gray clouds.

She couldn't see North Lake.

She couldn't see the Hollyberry Gardens.

Worst of all, she couldn't see Mount Wintersend.

"This is terrible," Maribel said. "If I can't see the kingdom, how will I know where to land?" She didn't know if she could accomplish her goal, but she did know one thing; if she failed, it could mean the worst for Callie. Maribel needed to help her friend return to good health. The safety of the kingdom and entire Island of Avonlea depended on it.

Maribel dove down through the clouds and flew against the storm. She turned her face away from the blizzard which threatened her mission. But as she flapped her magical feathered wings, wind spiraled in great gusts. The snow scattered, clearing a path, and allowing her a view of things in the distance. "Whoa!" she exclaimed. "My magic is more powerful than I ever knew! I can see so much more! In fact, that's Dreamsicle Pond right there."

Excited, she beat her wings faster, flying toward her destination. The cape whipped behind her as she sailed through the sky. Snow blew out of her way and Maribel nickered. "I'll shoot straight through this path, leaving the storm behind me. Then I'll find that flower and help my friend." She stretched her neck, pinning her ears and making her body straight as an arrow.

As she soared effortlessly, making a tunnel through the falling snow, Maribel squinted. "Mount Wintersend shouldn't be far now." She flapped her large, powerful wings. A clear path led straight to her destination. Soon a large peak came into view and Maribel's eyes widened. "That's it right there!" she neighed.

Snowflakes raced to the ground as she sped faster toward the great mountain range. Maribel needed to outpace the snow. She didn't know how long her magical wings could keep the path clear and open. If she hurried, she just might find her way to the flower that lay hidden somewhere between the mountains and water.

While she cruised through the storm, the cape billowing behind her, Maribel thought about Callie. How sad she felt knowing her friend was sick. Mending magic would be quite the undertaking. This flower was the only chance to help her friend. Maribel knew she had important work to do. She wouldn't let anyone down!

Maribel banked left toward the far end of the mountain range. The third highest peak was where the Three Friends Stream forked before reuniting at North Lake. That's where she'd find the flower. At least that's what King Hollyberry had told her. Maribel was sure she'd recognize the Meadowsweet flower from the image in the book. She just had to look for one stem with numerous blooms. Each tiny flower had five pointed petals all the color of snow. They also had a fluffy center like clouds. It was like nothing she'd ever seen before.

Soon she landed in the valley below Mount Wintersend. Maribel traipsed through the snow.

But the mounds were so dense and high it made walking difficult. Snow stuck to her body in thick clumps, and she shivered. She was grateful for Heidi's cloak as it kept some of the chill off, but she longed to be in front of a crackling fire.

With each step, Maribel grew more and more tired. The snow whipped her face and Maribel turned her head. "How will I ever find my way in this storm?" she chuffed. "It's much too difficult."

Maribel took a step, and her hoof sunk into the compacted snow. She glanced down and noticed that she was knee-deep. She could barely feel the ground beneath her hoof. That's when she realized the worst. "How will I find the flower if it's buried beneath all of this snow?"

A tear formed in the corner of Maribel's eye and as it rolled from her face, it froze into a tiny drop of ice. When the frozen tear hit the ground, it made a little circle in the snow. But soon the blizzard covered it with large flakes of white.

"The storm just keeps coming. There's absolutely no end in sight." Maribel glanced skyward, shaking her head. How could she save Callie if she couldn't locate that flower?

With a flap of her wings, Maribel sent the fresh snowflakes soaring. They spiraled away but as soon as she pulled her wings into her side, more snow simply took its place.

Maribel tipped her head. "I wonder...." She spread her magical wings and flapped them again, watching as the snow twisted and turned, blowing away in great waves. Just as it had when she was in flight, the snow reacted to the action of her wings.

"If I can control the wind with my wings, perhaps I can direct it another way." Maribel's eyes lit with excitement. "I have an idea and it may just work!"

Chapter 5

"The wind blows the snow away when I flap my magical wings. If I can direct the wind toward the ground, I might be able to move these mounds of snow. Then I may just find the flower!" Maribel reared up, waving her front hooves wildly with excitement.

She beat her wings with mighty power, guiding the wind toward a small area on the ground. But it didn't work. Snowflakes were light while they were in the air, but once they accumulated on the ground, it became a heavy and compact mound that was impossible to move.

"It's too dense," Maribel cried. "Not even my mighty wings can move the heaps of snow. It's as if I'm asking them to roll a boulder uphill."

Maribel shook her head. She felt defeated, but knew she had to keep trying. "What if I did it another way?" Maribel kicked the mound, breaking it into smaller pieces. She flapped her wings. Balls of snow rolled away. "That's it! It's going to work!"

The harder Maribel tried, the easier it became. She broke the dense mounds with her hooves, then flapped her wings. Soon the snow cleared completely from the spot, revealing tender stalks of grass. Maribel pranced through the little patch and into the snow, lifting her legs high. There was a spring in her step despite the bitter cold.

Maribel clomped through knee-deep mounds, breaking up the snow. She flapped her wings and sent the clumps soaring. But there was no flower. She marched to another spot and did the same. Still no flower. "This is a massive task," Maribel said as she realized how large the search would be. "The shoreline goes on forever. It could take all day!"

The blizzard turned everything white, including the patches Maribel had already cleared. She felt as though she may never find the flower. She turned in circles, wondering why the king had sent her on this impossible mission.

"What am I doing wrong?" Maribel cried. "King Hollyberry said I could find the flower where the Three Friends Stream meets at the shore of North Lake. But there's nothing here!"

Maribel looked at the streams. They joined together at the bank of North Lake, just as the king had said. "Wait a minute..." Maribel tipped her head. "Three streams, three intersections. Heavens to Avonlea!" she exclaimed, suddenly realizing an important detail. She was on the wrong side!

Maribel flapped her wings with such force that she lifted off the ground. Her back hooves brushed the freshly fallen snow as she leapt higher, her wings pulling her into the air.

Up.

Up.

Up.

Once Maribel was high above the land, she beat her wings and soared through the storm. When North Lake was directly beneath her, the pegacorn looped, and, gliding through the air, landed on the shore.

She stood on the opposite intersection of the Three Friends Stream and nodded. "I'm confident I'll find the blooms here! Then I'll fly back home and bring the cure to my friend."

Maribel stepped cautiously along the edge of the lake. Then, flapping her wings and pawing at the frozen land, Maribel searched for the Meadowsweet. She kept her face close to the ground, refusing to take her eyes off her work.

"It must be here," Maribel whispered. Her breath came out in a warm puff, making a cloud of white as it contacted the icy cold air. "I just know it."

With confidence, she pranced toward the stream. Maribel didn't see a patch of ice in her path and slipped. She stumbled from the shore and began sliding across the frozen lake.

"No, no, no!" Maribel cried. She stomped a hoof onto the slippery surface and spun to a stop. She heard a noise and looked down. A large crack had blossomed beneath her hoof. The fracture crept along the ice, growing larger and larger and splintering off in multiple directions.

Maribel slipped and slopped, struggling to regain her balance.

The sound of the breaking ice grew louder.

"I need to get out of here fast!" Maribel beat her wings, trying to steady her wobbly legs. She jetted into the air, hovering over the body of water. "Thank you, wings!" Maribel glanced down at the massive lake, the blizzard swirling everywhere around her. "That was a close one!" Without another thought, she flew back to shore.

"I must be more careful," Maribel said as she continued to hunt for the flower. As she stomped a hoof and flapped her wings, clearing her path, she saw something poking from the snow. "Is that what I think it is?" she said as she spied the star-shaped tips of the Meadowsweet.

Maribel hurried toward it. The pegacorn clomped her hoof into the mound. She stretched her powerful wings wide and flapped them with all the strength she had. The snow whirled away in great waves and clumps of white. Maribel dug carefully and broke up the remaining snow.

"The Meadowsweet flower!" Maribel exclaimed as she unearthed the bloom which had been cradled in the safety of snow. She couldn't believe she'd found it. She really did it! The flower was even more beautiful than the image in the book. Maribel quickly bent down and broke off one stem with her teeth. "You're just what I've been looking for!" she cried. But her words came out muffled as she clenched the flower between her lips.

Maribel didn't wait another second. She immediately lifted into the air and began to soar home. As she flew, she breathed in the sweet, nutty fragrance of the flower. Maribel felt sleepy and began to nod off. She shook her head and opened her eyes, forcing herself to stay awake. *I'm so tired*, she thought, tilting left and right, her flight taking on a wobbly path. *I can't seem to stay awake.* She fought against the sleep but soon it won. Maribel closed her eyes tight.

She dreamt of warm cocoa.

She dreamt of a crackling fire.

She dreamt of sweet treats and yummy food.

King Hollyberry's voice came to Maribel's mind. *"The flower has been known to cause a deep sleep."*

"Am I dreaming?" Maribel mumbled, half-awake. The pegacorn drowsily pried her eyes open. She blinked away the foggy film that had overtaken her.

When her eyes finally focused, Maribel saw the worst thing possible.

Maribel was spiraling out of control.

She plummeted.

Down.

Down.

Down.

Chapter 6

*M*aribel couldn't see anything through the storm. She had no idea of where she was or where she was headed. Then she heard a mighty growl.

"Is that what I think it is?" Maribel cried. Frightened, she flapped her wings, the snow clearing from her path. Beneath her was the scariest thing she'd ever seen. Maribel was headed straight toward a giant snow bear!

The bear's shaggy hair blew in the breeze as Maribel's flight spun out of control. Maribel plummeted downward and the bear stretched out its clawed hands. When the snow bear opened its mouth and exposed its large sharp teeth, it roared.

Maribel whinnied as she careened toward the fabled monster. She straightened her legs and stretched her wings wide, coming to a screeching halt. She hovered just above the snow bear's head as he swatted at the sky. Maribel beat her wings, lifting back up into the air. She then quickly banked left, making a sharp turn away from the snow bear.

"Another close one," she mumbled with the blooming stem still between her lips. *I must take care of this flower quickly. Can't have another mishap like that!* As soon as she reached safety, the snow bear long out of range, she landed softly in an open field.

Dropping the Meadowsweet flower on the snowy ground, Maribel shook her head. "I need to find a way to bring you to Callie. But your fragrance is making me so sleepy. There must be a way to keep me safe. Do you have any ideas?" Maribel stared at the flower, wondering how she would get it to her friend. "As if you can hear me." She giggled. "Now what can I use that will help?"

As Maribel folded her wings against her body, she gave a long, hard shake. Heidi's cape, which had kept her warm in this dangerous journey, billowed out around her. The fabric waved in the breeze, and Maribel had an idea. "Brilliant!" she whinnied. "I'll wrap you in the cape," she said to the flower. Then she pulled the ties with her teeth and the cloak fell to the ground. "The fabric will act as a barrier from your sleepy fragrance. But it will also protect you from the storm. It'll keep us both safe!"

As the snow continued to fall, Maribel swaddled the flower in the fabric and tied it up into a tight bundle. "That should do nicely," she said with a nod, then she picked the cloak up by its strings and clenched it tightly between her teeth. Battling the blizzard, she lifted into the sky, and soared straight through a path in the storm. When Callie's cottage came into view, Maribel swiftly landed. As she approached the house, she saw a very big problem.

Callie's front door was wide open.

This is very strange, Maribel thought. She dropped the swaddled flower on the ground. The house was quiet and dark, except for one light that shone out through a small, round window on the door. Callie's cottage lacked its usual warmth.

"An open door will let in a draft. That won't help Callie at all!" Maribel didn't understand how this could have happened. "Who would be so careless?"

"Not me," King Hollyberry said as he stepped out into the cold.

"Then who?" Maribel asked, wildly flapping her wings.

The door swung on its hinges, making great creaking sounds as it swayed back and forth.

Open. Shut.

Open. Shut.

Open. Shut.

Maribel flapped her wings.

Again, the door creaked back and forth.

"Who do you think?" King Hollyberry shook his head.

Maribel's eyes grew wide. She knew she could control the wind with her strong and magical wings. Had she made such powerful breezes that it blew Callie's door open? "Did I do that?" she whispered to herself.

"I believe so," King Hollyberry said with a grunt.

"I'm sorry," Maribel whinnied. While she knew of her great power, she hadn't always understood the impact it had on things around her. She should have been more careful!

Ignoring her own magic could cause harm and damage. In fact, she could accidentally blow the storm into a neighboring kingdom. If it reached Springsmorn, it would ruin the Sparkle Fruit Garden! If she blew the storm to the west, it would damage the Kingdom of Autumsneve. If she blew it south, it could chill the air in the Kingdom of Summerstart and create a frost on the colorful clovers.

Could Maribel be trusted with such a great power? After all, it could serve to do much damage. She wondered if someone more responsible should have been given this marvelous gift.

Her stomach twisted into knots and, without thinking, Maribel reared up and flapped her wings. Her carelessness could ruin the very island she loved.

"Must you do that?" The king shook his head as he pulled his robe tighter around himself. "You're creating an awful breeze!"

Even the king was upset. Maribel felt horrible. "What have I done?"

"No matter," King Hollyberry shouted into the wind. He gripped the knob, bracing himself against a large gust which threatened to take the door off its hinges. "I see you've made it back safely, Maribel. That's the important part. Now hurry before this draft causes us all to catch a chill!"

The king waved Maribel inside. But as Maribel stepped sideways, the king's eyes grew wide. "What is *this?*"

Maribel was afraid of upsetting him. "What do you mean, King Hollyberry?"

"Tell me what this is!" the king exclaimed, picking up the swaddling cloth containing the Meadowsweet flower and turning it over in his hands.

"That…that…that…" Maribel said with a shiver as she quickly crossed the threshold. The king used his shoulder to push the door shut. Before it fully closed, one snowflake snuck past, twirling inside. It spiraled down and a moment later melted away.

But King Hollyberry wasn't paying attention as he had already turned his back. He knelt on the floor and unfurled the cloak, revealing the Meadowsweet flower. "You've done it! By golly, you've really done it!"

"Why yes, I most certainly did." Maribel smiled, pleased with her accomplishment. She wasn't, however, about to tell the king she'd almost fallen asleep on her way home.

Or that she'd come dangerously close to a snow bear.

Or that she'd taken a scary spin on the frozen lake.

"The storm is getting worse. I fear for Avonlea if Callie isn't better soon." Maribel nudged the king's arm.

King Hollyberry gazed at Maribel, his expression growing serious. "You speak truth."

Maribel neighed. "There's no time to waste."

"Now then, let's put this to work!" The king marched off toward the kitchen and returned a moment later with a steaming mug of liquid. "Meadowsweet tea. If it does what the book promised, then it should work just like magic!"

Magic. Yes, that's exactly what they needed. More magic.

Magic to cure Callie's magic.

Maribel peered inside the mug where a single blossom floated in a bath of hot water and hollyberry syrup. "Hurry now! Bring it to Callie."

King Hollyberry scuttled off to Callie's room with the tea.

Maribel cantered to keep up, dodging a table with an unlit lamp. When she entered Callie's room, she saw her friend snuggled up under a pile of blankets with an ice pack on her head.

"I heard you weren't feeling well," Maribel said as she approached Callie's bedside.

"I feel awful," Callie said.

"Did you eat the soup that Heidi made?" Maribel asked.

Heidi, who had been standing at Callie's bedside, said, "She did! Every last bite."

"Good." Maribel nickered. "King Hollyberry has brought you something else. You must drink it. We want you to get better."

The king held the cup of Meadowsweet tea to Callie's lips. "It's hot, so be careful."

Callie took a sip of the tea. "It's delicious!"

She returned for a few more sips, and when she was finished, King Hollyberry placed the cup on Callie's bedside table. Soon Callie began to blink. Her head nodded, and she sighed.

"You should drink more," Heidi said, pushing the teacup closer. Her tail twitched and Heidi's eyes grew wide. "Hurry. You *must* finish it."

Callie rested her head on a fluffy pillow trimmed with a large white ruffle. "I'm too tired," she said with a yawn. Her eyelids fluttered before they finally closed, and Callie drifted off to sleep.

"Then you should rest. Sweet dreams, Callie." Maribel looked over at the king with a smile and whispered, "It works quickly, doesn't it?" If only Maribel had known how fast it brought on sleep, she would have practiced more caution with it on her flight.

"It certainly does." The king nodded, pulled the covers up, and tucked Callie back in.

The storm blew past a large window beside Callie's bed. It overlooked the yard but the only thing visible was more snow. Except for a little red bird who sat shivering on the outside ledge of the windowsill.

"Can I come in?" the bird asked.

Callie stretched, lifted her head, and peeked out from under the blankets. "Noelle?" she mumbled groggily. But as quickly as she had stirred, she fell back to sleep again. A little wad of drool dripped from her mouth.

"Yes, it's me!" The bird ruffled her red feathers. The snow came down so heavily that she was instantly covered in white.

King Hollyberry unlatched the window, and Noelle flew inside. A flurry of snow followed her, blowing into the room. Callie shivered, and the king quickly pushed the window closed. He brushed the freshly fallen snow from Callie's bedside table.

"It's so cold out there," Noelle tweeted. "Is it going to stop snowing soon?"

"That's what we're trying to solve now," Maribel said.

Noelle flew over to Callie, landing on the top of her horn. "What more is there to know? Callie controls winter and only she can make it stop. Isn't that right, Callie?" Noelle bent over, looking at the sleeping pegacorn.

"She's sick," Heidi said. She nudged the teacup which sat on the bedside table.

Noelle gasped. "Oh, my! I didn't realize she was under the weather."

"She'll be feeling better soon." Maribel rubbed her muzzle against the king's shoulder. "Thanks to the efforts of Heidi and King Hollyberry."

"Don't be silly now, Maribel. I'm certain it wasn't anything I did." The king patted Maribel's head. Then he turned toward the red bird and said, "It was Maribel who did the hard work. She braved the blizzard to find a cure; the Meadowsweet flower."

Maribel blushed. "And I'd do it again."

"That was very thoughtful of you," Noelle said with a tweet. "But I'm afraid it may not work fast enough."

"What do you mean?" King Hollyberry retreated to the corner of the room. He lowered himself into a chair—one that was two sizes too small—and groaned.

"She's right! There's so much snow," Heidi said as she gazed out the fogged-up window, flicking her tail. "It's falling faster than I've ever seen before."

"Callie will be well soon enough and then the snow will stop," Maribel said with a neigh.

Noelle twittered toward Maribel and landed on the pegacorn's back, right between her wings. "But I'm afraid you don't understand—"

The door burst open and Paisley, a pega-corn with a white-gray coat, trotted in. Paisley's mane and tale were the softest and palest shade of green, like lichen-covered tree bark, a type of soft green moss that grew on the trees only seen in Springsmorn.

Paisley reared up on her hind legs. "The snow!" she cried. Normally Paisley was known to be calm, so it was a little surprising to see her here with such excitement. She flapped her sparkly wings, sending a slight breeze across the room.

"Yes, there's lots of snow," Maribel said.

The king strummed his fingers on the arm of the chair. "Callie isn't well."

"We're here to help her recover," Heidi said.

Paisley flapped her wings again. "The… snow…" Paisley panted between words.

Maribel nodded. "We know."

Paisley shook her head. "I don't think you understand."

"It's what I've been trying to tell them," Noelle tweeted, fluttering over to perch on Paisley's crystal horn.

Noelle and Paisley shouted in unison, "The storm is headed to Autumnseve!"

"*I* knew it!" Heidi turned toward her tail which twitched again. "Don't worry. We won't let that happen."

"We can't allow our friends to get hurt," Maribel cried. "That would be tragic!"

King Hollyberry stared wide-eyed at Maribel. "Something must be done to stop this."

"Maybe someone should warn them," Paisley said with a whinny. "Perhaps if someone talks to the dragons, they can spread the word. Given enough time, they can prepare for the storm."

Heidi lowered her head. "What about the unicorns in the Kingdom of Autumnseve? Even if the dragons could prepare, they can't stop the storm. Only Callie can do that. What would the unicorns do once the blizzard reaches them?"

"They'd need to save the Purple Pumpkin Patch. It would be ruined!" Paisley shook her head, and her fluffy mane looked like a puff of cotton candy.

"That's true. The pumpkins may be able to withstand frost but definitely not snow." Maribel began to pace in front of the window. She pinned her ears and neighed. "Morgan would be terribly upset to see her pumpkins ruined. You know how hard she works."

"And we wouldn't have any treats for the coming year." Paisley pranced over to Maribel. She quickly fell in step and the two paced shoulder-to-shoulder, their hooves clip-clopping against the floor.

Maribel thought about the terrible things that could happen if the snowstorm continued to spiral out of control. She wondered if she had caused the storm to drift into the next kingdom. Had her powerful and magical wings changed the course of the storm the way it had blown the door open on Callie's house? Impossible! Her wings weren't strong enough to do that. Or were they?

If this was her fault, Maribel needed to do everything she could to stop it. "Then there's no choice. I must go warn them." She retrieved Heidi's cloak. She picked it up with her teeth and carried it to the king.

"Are you sure it's safe?" Heidi asked with a flick of her tail.

"Maribel is strong and powerful. You saw how she returned without issue last time. I've no doubt she'll do the same now," King Holly-berry said to Heidi. Then he threw the silver-trimmed cloak over Maribel's back. He gave Maribel a pat on her withers and whispered in her ear, "You'll do just fine."

Maribel nickered as she trotted toward the

door. "I promise. I'll go quickly and return. But you must assure me you'll keep watch over Callie. She needs to recover. I'm not sure how much longer the kingdom will hold out."

"You can count on us," the pegacorns and King Hollyberry said in unison, their voices a choir of colorful sound.

"Then I'll be on my way." Maribel crossed out into the blizzard, lifted her head to the sky, and closed her eyes. Snowflakes landed on her eyelashes, and she blinked them away. "To Autumnseve!"

"To Autumnseve!" the friends chorused.

"Be safe," Paisley called out.

The snow came down heavily, but Maribel quickly lifted into the sky. She soared high above Wintersend.

While Maribel knew the storm was headed toward the neighboring kingdom, she had hoped to outpace it and eventually fly through clear skies. Unfortunately, that wasn't the case. Whiteout conditions still blurred her path.

"I've only one choice," Maribel said. "I'll push the wind with my magical wings. That will chase the snow from my path as it did before." She flapped her wings, but she was so tired and weak that the snow refused to obey. "It's no use. Not even my powerful wings can help me."

Maribel needed to warn the dragons, but the task seemed impossible. She had used all her strength to find the Meadowsweet flower and now she couldn't clear the path.

As she flew through the sky, Maribel struggled to see beyond her nose. She worried she hadn't gone far enough. Then she feared she'd gone too far. If she'd flown past Dragonfire Forest, then she'd be lost out at Dragon Sea. Maribel didn't know what lay beyond the large body of water, and she was sure she never wanted to find out.

Maribel worried she might get lost. Not only would that be terrible for her, but it would mean disaster for all of Avonlea. Maribel was their only hope to warn the dragons about the storm.

If I can't see where I'm headed, Maribel thought to herself, *how will I know when I've reached Dragonfire Forest?*

Snow twirled all about and Maribel became dizzy. The world swiveled and swirled around her. The cold, crisp, snowy air bit at her face. Her flight felt out of control, and she struggled to steady her wings.

"Be calm," Maribel whispered to herself as she closed her eyes. "No need to panic. Just breathe. Focus. Soon you'll find your way."

Then Maribel felt something wonderful.

A tingling in her hooves.

A warmth in her horn.

A calm and steady assurance.

Just let your senses guide you. Your wings have never steered you wrong. You must believe and trust. You've flown it many times before.

Maribel took a deep breath. Soon the images of the path came to her mind. She could see the entire route. It was as clear to her as a cloudless sky. "I know the way! It's to the left," Maribel said with her eyes still closed as she flapped her wings. "Just a little further, I believe."

When she opened her eyes, she whinnied with excitement at what she saw.

No more snow.

No more gray skies.

She'd outflown the storm!

Chapter 9

"I did it!" Maribel cried with joy. "And look! Just there!" She lowered her head, gazing at the flickering leaves below. "It's Dragonfire Forest!"

Maribel swooped down feeling the warmth of the fire leaves on her face while the cold storm pressed against her back. She landed in the Kingdom of Autumnseve and galloped toward Dragonfire Forest.

"Grandfather Merlin! Come quickly!" Maribel panted out the words.

A large green dragon crept between trees before crawling from the forest. "What is it, small unicorn?" Grandfather Merlin towered over Maribel. He glanced down at her and blinked. Then he coughed, and a little spark shot from his mouth. "Pardon. I'm mistaken. I mean pegacorn. Shouldn't you be in Wintersend?"

Maribel lowered her front legs and bowed. "I've come to warn you."

"Warn *me*? Why on Avonlea would you be warning *me*?" Grandfather Merlin huffed and flared his large nostrils. He turned and, looking at the pegacorn with a nod, said, "There's a great storm brewing."

"That's right! How'd you know?" Maribel stretched her wings, gave a gentle flap, and then folded them in at her sides.

"Winds of change told me." Plumes of smoke spiraled out of the dragon's nose and were soon swept away by the incoming storm.

Maribel watched as the smoke floated out to Dragon Sea. "Can the winds of change tell you how severe it is?"

"Perhaps." Grandfather Merlin nodded. He then licked a claw and held it to the wind. "Hmmm...well...that is bad," he said with a groan. "Now, why don't you tell me why you're here."

"I've come to warn you about the storm, but I see you already know." Maribel looked up at the great dragon who stood as tall as the trees. "Callie is sick, and the storm is out of control. It won't stop snowing, and the

Kingdom of Wintersend is nearly buried. As you know, it's headed your way, and we fear it will cause an unspeakable amount of trouble."

"Is that so?" The dragon turned his head toward the northern kingdom and took a deep sniff of air. "You've spoken truth. This is quite the storm," he said with a nod.

"Then you must hurry. Please help the unicorns in Autumnseve and keep the kingdom safe." Maribel cantered in a circle, feeling a bit anxious.

"You have my word," Grandfather Merlin said. He crouched down and studied the pegacorn. "Have you regained your strength?"

Maribel's eyes grew wide. "Whatever do you mean?" How did Grandfather Merlin know her wings had grown weak? Could he also know if she had blown the storm here by mistake?

"Never fear. You're not at fault." Grandfather Merlin stood back up, closed his eyes and nodded. He sniffed deeply and blinked. "I do believe your strength is restored. Your magic, however, is another matter," he said with a wink.

"My...my magic?" Maribel worried that maybe her magic was broken, too.

"Hush now. It's not time for such questions," Grandfather Merlin said. Then he lifted his giant clawed hand and snapped his fingers. The small flicker of flames that lit the treetops grew to a roaring fire.

Maribel gasped. "Won't you burn down the forest?"

"Nonsense!" Grandfather Merlin laughed. "We have it completely under control. Don't we boys?" As Grandfather Merlin turned away, a flight of mighty dragons gathered behind him.

The dragons all roared in unison, and Maribel took a step back. She'd never heard such a fearsome noise before. She wondered if the unicorns in Autumnseve feared the dragons. Perhaps, instead, they felt protected by them. Maribel wasn't sure how she would feel if dragons lived in her kingdom. She had been frightened enough by a snow bear.

A blue dragon with large leather-like wings stood up. He was so tall that his head was nearly level with Grandfather Merlin's. "What have you to say for yourself?" he roared.

Maribel bucked, kicking her hooves up. She came down hard, neighing loudly and flapping her wings.

"Don't be afraid," the dragon said. "My name is Percival and I only want the story."

"It's the storm," Maribel said, trying to hide the tremble in her voice. "Callie is sick, and her magic is broken. Until we can help her recover, we all need to work together to protect the island."

"We'll take care of things here." Percival looked up at the sky, which was darkening quickly. "Now hurry! There's no time to waste.

You must return to your kingdom and help your friend."

"I assure you I'll do whatever it takes," Maribel said.

Percival ducked into the forest. The dragons then slithered and creeped about in the woods, each heading in a different direction. One breathed ice from his large mouth and another changed shape.

"Whoa," Maribel whispered. "I didn't know the dragons could shape-shift."

"We can become invisible, too," a voice hissed in her ear.

Maribel whirled around, and a purple dragon took shape before her.

"Lancelot's my name, invisibility is my game," he whispered before disappearing again.

"Strange and marvelous creatures," Maribel nickered. She watched them a moment longer, then thought, *my job here is done. Now I must return to my kingdom.*

Suddenly, the blizzard blew in, flakes of snow chasing each other. The fire leaves flickered. Maribel would have to fight hard to fly against that storm. It would be exhausting but she believed she could do it. She steadied and braced herself.

There was little time left.

She had only one choice.

Maribel flew straight into the storm.

Chapter 10

"Oh no," Maribel said as she flew into the blizzard. Snow came down in heavy sheets of white. The cloudy skies of Wintersend and the accompanying cold air chilled her to the bone. The silver-trimmed cloak was of little comfort as she shivered to stay warm.

As Maribel flew toward Callie's house, she dreamed of warming herself by a toasty fire. She'd had two incredible journeys today, and she longed to rest. But first things first. She needed to follow through with her promise and help her friend.

The storm pressed at Maribel's face. But she felt a surge of strength, just as Grandfather Merlin had assured, and the snow was no match for her mighty wings. Maribel soared effortlessly through the blizzard, pushing the snow away and clearing a path.

"Silly dragon, playing tricks on me,"

Maribel said with a chuckle. "I knew my magic wasn't broken. Just look at how strong my wings are."

As she circled above her kingdom, Maribel saw a soft orange glow of lights. "I'm almost there. Just a little further." When Callie's house came into view, Maribel gave one very large and very strong flap, changed direction— swooping down toward the snow-covered ground—and landed in a mound of the cold, white powder.

"Look at how much it's snowed in the short time I was away," Maribel whinnied. The snow had passed her knees and reached her chest. She tried to rear up, but she could barely move her legs. "This is terrible. Absolutely dreadful."

Maribel glanced at the door, which felt so out of reach. "What can I do now? The door is nearly blocked by all of the snow." She squinted one eye and peeked into the little round window on the door. A soft orange glow lit the inside of the house as a fire roared in the front room. "It looks so cozy," she said with a shiver. "What I wouldn't give to warm myself."

"What are you doing out there?" a voice cried. Heidi's face popped into view. Her cheeks were rosy, and she looked so warm and cozy inside the house.

Maribel longed to warm herself inside. She chuffed and her breath fogged the window.

Suddenly, the door burst open. "Come in, come in! You'll catch cold," King Hollyberry said. He held the door, and the mound of snow collapsed, freeing Maribel. She trotted across the threshold. With the help of Heidi and Paisley, King Hollyberry promptly swept the snow out of the way and pushed the door closed.

"You must be freezing," Paisley said.

"I was. Thanks for letting me in." Maribel shook the snow from her cloak which melted into little puddles as soon as it hit the warm wood floor.

"Were you able to bring the message to the dragons?" Heidi asked. Her tail twitched and she smiled.

"They were glad I came, but I think Grandfather Merlin would have known without me," Maribel said.

"Why do you believe that?" The king removed the silver-trimmed cloak from Maribel's back. He turned and hung it on a hook by the door.

Maribel remembered Grandfather Merlin's actions, how he seemed to sense and smell the storm. "Just a hunch," she said.

"Thank you for your courage." King Hollyberry patted Maribel's back. "I'm afraid Callie isn't any better than before." With a shake of his head, the king sighed and sunk into a chair.

"That's terrible," Maribel walked toward the fire and warmed herself by the flames. "We must find a way to get her better before things get any worse."

"We've already tried everything," Paisley said as she tossed her mane. The soft, bouncy lichen-colored hair fell gently against her face. "What can we do?"

"There's nothing more that can be done," Heidi said. "We have to trust Callie will get better. Her magic must be restored."

"Of course, she will get well," the king said. "We've never doubted that."

"The problem isn't if she will recover, but if she'll do it before it's too late," Paisley said as she looked out the window. "Soon we'll be buried under all that snow! There isn't much time."

"Not only that, but the other kingdoms could face trouble, too." Maribel tapped her hooves and the melted snow, which had collected in little puddles, splashed from the stone hearth to the wood floor.

King Hollyberry wiped up the water with a towel. "Avonlea may very well be ruined."

Maribel nodded. She knew that there was a delicate balance on the island. Avonlea was their home. The unicorns and pegacorns had a responsibility to maintain it.

"We must find another way," Maribel said as she turned her back to the hearth. "And I know just what we need to do."

Chapter 11

"*We* need to wake her." Maribel marched straight into Callie's room. She gasped when she saw Callie already standing at the bedside, rocking on wobbly legs. "What are you doing out of bed?"

"What do you mean?" With a turn of her head, Callie looked back at where she'd been sleeping for the last several hours. "I'm not sure."

"Are you feeling well?" Maribel asked, approaching her friend.

"I believe so." Callie blinked, yawned, then gave a satisfied chuff. "Why yes. I feel so much better!" she exclaimed. "Wait…was I sick?"

"It worked!" Maribel neighed. "It really worked!"

Callie swayed, looking a little dizzy. "What did?"

"Whoa, steady," Maribel said as she rushed to Callie's side. "It was the Meadowsweet flower. But it appears as though you're still weak. Maybe you should rest a little longer." As she helped Callie under the covers, the cup of tea at the bedside clattered to the floor. It shattered into pieces, making quite the ruckus.

Paisley, Heidi, and King Hollyberry rushed into the room.

"Is everything all right?" the king asked.

Callie sat up. "King Hollyberry! What are you doing here?"

"She's cured!" Heidi whinnied.

"You're all better!" Paisley said.

Callie stumbled out of bed, looking confused and a little worse for wear. "What's all the commotion? What's happened?"

"You don't remember?" the king asked as he approached the pegacorn.

"I feel awfully confused." Callie shook her head, strands of her long lavender-colored mane falling into her eyes.

"It's a side-effect of the flower." King Hollyberry crossed an arm and rested his chin in the palm of his other hand. "It'll wear off shortly," he said.

"What is going on?" Callie stumbled

toward the footboard, swaying on wobbly legs. "Please tell me."

"Maybe you should see for yourself." Maribel stared out the bedroom window watching the snow fall.

The blizzard blew past the glass in sheets of white. "Oh my!" Callie gasped. "Did I make all that snow?"

"You could say that." Heidi neighed.

Callie turned toward Maribel with wide eyes. Then she looked at Heidi, Paisley, and King Hollyberry. "So *that's* why you're all here."

"Precisely," King Hollyberry said as he glanced out the window. "And your friend Maribel risked everything to find the cure."

"You did that for me?" Callie chuffed.

"And I'd do it again," Maribel said.

Callie glanced at the floor and back up at her friend. "How can I ever repay you?"

"That won't be necessary," Maribel said. "But we do need you to stop this storm."

"And fast!" Heidi said.

Callie blinked. "Of course, of course." She reared up, her front hooves waving wildly, and little sparks of silver trickled out. Another tiny spark came from her horn. They all fizzled out quickly, and soon Callie began to sway on her hind legs, looking quite dizzy. Her front hooves came back down, landing with a loud thud. She stumbled but quickly regained her footing. "I think my magic is broken!"

"She's still too weak," the king said. He shook his head and mumbled something to himself.

"I know it's hard," Maribel whispered.

"But you've taken on much harder tasks in the past. Remember when you were afraid to fly?"

Callie fluttered her eyes with a nod. "How could I forget?"

"But you conquered your fears." Maribel shook her long, silvery-blue mane. "You flew!"

"No, she didn't," Heidi said, giving Paisley a little nod. The two smiled.

Maribel glanced at the grinning pair. "They're right you know. You didn't fly."

"I most certainly did so," Callie said as she set her shoulders. "I flew high above the kingdom."

"No. No you didn't." Maribel winked. "You *soared*."

"I did, didn't I?" Callie neighed loudly, tipping her head back. With a whisper, she said, "I soared higher than any pegacorn in the history of Avonlea."

"But that's not all," Maribel said.

"Nope!" Heidi's voice tinkled like a bell.

Paisley pawed a hoof at the floor. "There's more!"

"So much more!" Maribel chuffed

Callie whinnied. "I think I know the answer!"

"And what's that?" Maribel brushed her shoulder against Callie's.

"I saved winter," Callie whispered.

"That's right!" Maribel smiled at her dear friend. "And you can do it again."

Callie's voice was weak as she hung her head. "I'm afraid I can't."

"But you must." Paisley swished her tail and the soft, fluffy hair bounced like clouds. "You're the only one who can stop this storm. If you don't, the kingdom will soon be buried beneath all that snow."

"My magic is broken." Callie trotted out of the room, crying.

The friends followed the pegacorn of winter into the living room where the crackling fire warmed the space with an orange glow.

"That may be true for now." Paisley stood in front of the window, looking out into the yard, her breath fogging up the glass. "But it won't always be that way. Your magic will mend, and then you can put an end to all of this snow!"

King Hollyberry stood next to Paisley stroking his long, white beard. "Only time will tell."

"But we can't wait much longer." Heidi trotted closer to the fire and gazed into the flames.

"Heidi is right," Maribel said. "You must try, Callie. The storm is already approaching Dragonfire Forest."

"That would be a disaster!" Callie's eyes grew wide. "What have I done?"

"It's not your fault," Maribel said. "But you can certainly be the cure."

Heidi kept her eyes on the fire, not blinking, as her tail swished to and fro. "I'm afraid things will get much worse before they get better."

"What makes you think that?" Maribel asked.

"Just a twitch I've got in my tail." With that, Heidi flicked her orange tail and darted into the kitchen.

A chill crept down Maribel's back. She had never known Heidi to be wrong, especially when her tail got its special little twitch. If Heidi was right, then Avonlea was headed for disaster.

"Do you think you can try again?" Maribel asked Callie. "The kingdom can't withstand much more snow. If the storm really does blow into Autumnseve, it could ruin much more than we feared."

"The Purple Pumpkin Patch will be destroyed," Paisley said.

Maribel shook her head, wishing she had done more to help. What if the dragons didn't follow through? "There's no telling what may happen to our unicorn friends."

"Please try. Just one more time." Paisley pressed her nose against Callie's shoulder. "Your magic can't stay broken forever."

"You're right," Callie said with a nod. She

put her head down and closed her eyes. She pinched her lips together. Sparks began to sputter from her horn.

"Keep going! You can do it!" Maribel neighed as she watched her friend's magic flicker to life.

Callie flapped her wings. She began to lift off the ground. More sparks came out of her horn. Then smaller sparkles appeared from her hooves.

"Hurry," Paisley said, rushing toward the front of the cottage. "I'll open the door!"

Without blinking, Callie flew out into the cold, snowy kingdom.

"She's going to do it!" Maribel cried as she rushed through the doorway. "She's going to stop the storm!"

Callie soared through the blizzard. Although her coat of white made it difficult to find her within the storm, the clouds soon began to break. Little slivers of blue sky appeared among the thick gray clouds.

"There she is!" Maribel shouted as she spotted Callie's iridescent hooves.

"You can do it, Callie!" Paisley said as she reared back.

After making multiple loops in the sky, Callie soared back down. Her wings shimmered, looking as magical as her special gift. Callie landed gracefully and trotted through the mounds of snow until she reached the front door. She ruffled her feathered wings, shook her mane, and cantered inside.

Paisley cheered. "That was magnificent, Callie!" Her eyes were wide with wonder as she greeted the pegacorn of winter.

"Thank you," Callie said with a bow.

Maribel looked skyward. Although a few more patches of blue began to appear, snow still flurried from the remaining clouds.

"I hope it worked." Paisley rubbed noses with Callie.

Callie giggled. "Shall I go and try again?"

"No need. Just look!" Maribel pointed a hoof toward the window. "The snow has stopped!"

"Heavens to Avonlea! It really did work!" Heidi cried with joy. She scowled at her tail, then gave it one good flick. "This is one time I'm glad you were wrong."

Maribel chuckled, then turned to see King

Hollyberry rushing toward Callie with his arms wide open.

"You did it!" the king exclaimed, hugging the pegacorn of winter.

"We all did," Callie said. "We worked together."

"That's right," Paisley said. "Maribel fought the storm to find the flower."

"Had she not been brave enough to do that, we could all still be in danger." Heidi's tail began to twitch, and she spun in circles, chasing it. "You were wrong. Now stop with your silly predictions and hush!" Her tail swung slowly in place.

"Maribel also warned the dragons." King Hollyberry patted Maribel on the back. "You're strong and brave."

"My *wings* are strong," Maribel said with a blush. "I couldn't have made it through the storms without them."

"Thanks to teamwork, Avonlea will be saved!" Callie exclaimed.

Everyone cheered.

"Now that you're feeling better, Callie, perhaps it's time for us all to return home,"

Maribel said. "I'm exhausted and could use a nice, long rest."

The little red bird, Noelle, flew into view. She tapped on the window with her beak. "Let me in, please," she tweeted. "There's something I must tell you."

"What seems to be the matter?" Maribel unlatched the window.

Noelle flew inside and darted from the mantel to a lamp and back to the mantel. "It's Wintersend!" she chirped.

"Isn't it spectacular?" Paisley asked with a swish of her tail. "The snow has finally stopped!"

"Thanks to Callie who saved the day." Maribel clopped her hooves on the floor and chuffed.

Noelle bobbed her head. "I understand, but—"

"I didn't do it alone," Callie said.

"That's true." Heidi began to flick her tail. "It really was all of us."

Callie turned and nodded. "I couldn't have done it without you, Maribel."

Heidi chimed in again. "Maribel found the flower and—"

"Stop!" Noelle's head swiveled as she looked from one pegacorn to the next. "Please stop!"

"What's wrong?" Maribel asked.

"What seems to be the problem?" Heidi said with a neigh.

"Just look!" Noelle pointed her feathered wing toward the window.

The clouds had disappeared.

The snow had stopped.

They both had been replaced with sunshine, warm and bright like a day in Summerstart.

The ground, no longer covered in deep mounds of snow, revealed something troublesome. Green grass, rarely seen in Wintersend, poked out of the soil. Worse, the melted snow had become water. And it looked like trouble.

"What's this?" Maribel blinked.

The bird chirped loudly. "It's a flood!"

*M*aribel reared up on her hind legs. "How is that possible?" Her hooves came down with a loud clap of thunder.

"My magic is still broken!" Callie gasped. "I didn't mean to melt the snow."

Heidi trotted over to the window and peeked outside. "Heavens to Avonlea! This is terrible."

"Now that the snow has melted, it has turned to water. It has no choice but to run downhill." King Hollyberry threw his arms up with a huff. He retrieved his staff that had been tucked beside the mantel. Then he rocked on his heels while strumming his fingers on his staff.

"Which means it's headed straight to North Lake." Paisley trotted over to the window and rubbed shoulders with Heidi.

"Just look at how fast that water is

running!" Heidi neighed. "It's faster than Rainbow River!"

"The dam at North Lake wasn't meant to hold that much water. It'll burst if we don't stop it." Maribel squeezed between her friends and peered out of the window. "If the dam breaks, our friends in the other kingdoms will be in danger." She felt helpless as she realized the depth of the problem.

Heidi nipped at her twitching tail. "It might even run toward Glitter Palace. Should we warn Guinevere and Genevieve?"

As King Hollyberry paced in front of the hearth, his forehead dripped with sweat. "No, no. There's a moat surrounding the castle. The twins will be just fine."

"But we must save the others on the island," Noelle said with a tweet.

Maribel fell in step with the king and the pair paced the room. Flicking her tail, Maribel lowered her head. "How will we ever manage that?"

"The only way is to mend my magic." Callie ruffled the feathers on her large, white wings and quickly tucked them against her body.

"That's right. Callie's the only one who can control the snow." Heidi's hooves clip-clopped on the floor as she paced alongside Maribel and the king. "Can you make it snow again?"

"No!" King Hollyberry exclaimed with his eyes wide. "No more snow."

Callie winced. "I'm sorry to have caused so much trouble."

"Don't you worry, friend," Noelle said as she settled in Callie's lavender mane.

"We'll solve this together." Maribel glanced at Callie, who frowned and lowered her head.

Paisley stood looking out the window. "But snow would stop the flood."

"It's snow that's caused the problem in the first place." Heidi flicked her tail, just missing Paisley's hindquarters.

Maribel squinted at them. "There must be

another solution."

"Good point," Paisley said. "We must find an option that doesn't require Callie's magic. At least until we know it's completely mended."

The king nodded. "That's an excellent point."

"We can always hope that the water will run off into the Dragon Sea. Then there will be nothing to worry about. We won't need magic to help us then." Maribel chuffed as she stopped suddenly and peeked out the window. For the first time since she could remember, the glass didn't fog up. Which reminded her of how cold and snowy it had been. She thought maybe the snow was better than all this water. What a mess they were in!

"By golly, that's it!" The king leapt up, tossing his crown toward the ceiling. It twirled around before landing perfectly on top of his head.

"What is?" Maribel stepped back, watching the king's excitement.

"We need to enlist the help of someone else." King Hollyberry danced and spun in circles around the room. "Di-dee, diddly-dee, I know who it should be!"

Chapter 14

*H*eidi trotted toward the king. Her
tail twitched with that special
little jolt. "Who do you think we should ask?"

"Maeve!" the king exclaimed. "She controls
water!"

"That's a brilliant idea!" Heidi neighed as
she pranced around the room.

Paisley flapped her wings. "Splendid! I
knew we'd find a solution."

"Why didn't I think of that?" Maribel
watched the melted snow run like great rivers
through the kingdom.

"Do you really think Maeve could help?"
Callie asked. She raised her head as Noelle
hopped to the tip of Callie's horn.

"I most certainly do." King Hollyberry
stroked his beard. His forehead wrinkled and
his lips were pinched in a line. He grumbled
with a huff. "But how can we ask for Maeve's
help?"

"I could fly to the Kingdom of Springsmorn." Paisley lifted a hoof to volunteer. "I'm swift and sure. It would take me no time at all to arrive there."

"You *are* the fastest in the kingdom," Maribel said thoughtfully. "But Maeve doesn't have wings. Once you've found her, she'd have to walk here and that would take much too long."

"We could use a sled." Heidi's eyes grew wide as her tail twitched. "Hush now. No more out of you," she whispered as she turned in a circle, nipping at her tail.

King Hollyberry nodded. "That may just work."

"Then we have a solution!" Heidi reared up in excitement. "Avonlea will be saved!"

"Not so fast," Maribel said, turning her attention to the window. "We have an even bigger problem on our hands."

"What's that?" King Hollyberry hustled over to Maribel. The king looked outside and gasped. "The snow has melted from the mountains and come into the valley. The flood waters are rising!"

"Now do you see what I mean?" Maribel

asked. "Avonlea will be under water before we could even get to Maeve. It would be too late."

"We must find a solution quickly." King Hollyberry removed the book from his robe and pushed his sleeves up. "Do you have another idea?"

Paisley tapped her hooves on the floor, prancing in excitement. "I have one!"

"Tell us," Heidi exclaimed.

"Perhaps we could fly to each of the kingdoms and warn them." Paisley squared her withers and held her head high.

"I can help," Noelle tweeted.

King Hollyberry furrowed his brow then glanced down at the book. "How would that stop the flood?"

"Well, it wouldn't exactly, but two kingdoms have mountains. If we can get everyone to higher ground, they'll be safe," Paisley said with a smile.

"It's an excellent idea!" Heidi nodded but her tail still twitched. "We could wait out the flood in safety."

"Not so fast," Maribel said, looking between her friends. "It might keep us safe, but what about the dragons and all of the other creatures who live on the island? And what about the crops? A flood would ruin the food." Maribel feared what would happen to them. She spread her wings, flapping them fast.

The king squinted as the gust of wind flipped the pages of his leather-bound book. "This is true," he mumbled as he stilled the pages with his hand. "Maribel has made an excellent point. There'd be no food left for anyone."

Heidi's eyes grew wide. "We'd all go hungry."

Paisley frowned. "I thought it was a good idea, but I can see that it wouldn't be much help."

"There must be another way," Noelle chirped.

Maribel whinnied. "This can't be the end of Avonlea."

King Hollyberry clapped the book shut and tucked it back into his sleeve. He groaned as he began to pace again. "There weren't any answers in my book." The king's robe dragged on the floor behind him. It snagged on a nail and he stumbled forward.

Startled, Maribel flapped her wings, stirring a large gust of wind. "Are you hurt?"

"Fine, fine." King Hollyberry turned away with a shiver. "I'm quite all right."

Maribel helped the king to his feet, flapping her wings to steady herself. "I wish we could find a way to save the island from the flood."

"We must keep thinking," King Hollyberry said, brushing dust from his robe.

"We're overlooking something." Maribel reared up, feeling a sense of urgency. She flapped her wings, stirring up a breeze so fierce that the curtains hanging on either side of the window began to billow into the room.

"Must you make such a gust?" King Hollyberry cried, shielding his face with his arms.

"Too much wind," Heidi neighed as her mane blew into her eyes.

"This isn't the time for such a breeze." Paisley dug her hooves into the floor. She braced herself against the gust that threatened to send her sailing across the room.

"I'm sorry," Maribel brought her hooves back down and folded her wings close to her side. She wasn't always aware of how her strong wings affected others.

"Don't be sorry," King Hollyberry said. "Just be more careful."

"I'll try." Maribel didn't want to feel sad, but they were all in danger, and it seemed her carelessness could have made things much worse.

"But..." Heidi looked back and forth between the king and Maribel. "Don't you see?"

"See what?" Maribel asked, watching the flood roll by outside. She rustled the feathers of her wings, shaking a small breeze across the room.

"That! That right there!" Heidi exclaimed.

Paisley blinked. "I see what you mean!"

The king's eyes grew wide. "Why of course!" he exclaimed. "How could I have missed it?"

"Missed what?" Maribel asked, still looking out the window.

"You!" The king danced around the room, his robe and beard swaying with each little jump of his jig. "You, diddly do, do, YOU!"

"Me?" Maribel turned sharply. "Did I do something wrong?"

"On the contrary," Heidi said with a giggle. "You did everything right!"

"I did?" Maribel felt very confused. She had no idea of what was happening and why her friends thought she was responsible.

"Yes, you did," the king said, continuing to dance a jig around the room.

"What did I do?" Maribel raised her feathered wings, and gave one single flap, sending the curtains fluttering in the wind.

"That!" Heidi neighed.

"The breeze?" Maribel squinted at her friend.

"Your wings make the strongest breezes in all of Wintersend." King Hollyberry held Maribel's face in his hands and looked straight into her eyes. "They just might be strong enough to stop the flood."

"*D*o you really think so?" Maribel reared up on her hind legs, flapping her wings. Wind whipped around the room, sweeping upward then down as it twisted and turned in a magical dance.

"I do believe so," Heidi said.

King Hollyberry placed his hands on his hips. "We must put an end to this flood. And you're just the pegacorn to do it!"

"I wish with all my heart that I could stop the flood," Maribel said. "I'll try my very best."

"Did you call?" A beautiful fairy fluttered just outside the window.

Maribel stared wide-eyed with her mouth agape. "Me?"

"Yes, you. Now, must I wait for you to let me in, or shall I do it myself?" The fairy tapped the wand against the window, and it opened in a flash. She floated inside, patted

Maribel's head, and landed gracefully on her tiptoes.

"Who are you?" Maribel gasped.

"I'm Fairy Princess Windgust and I'm here to grant your wish." The fairy twirled around, showing off her beautiful fur-trimmed cloak. Her long dark hair was twisted into two braids that framed both sides of her face.

King Hollyberry smiled. "Well, well! Fairy Princess Windgust, it's nice to have you join us."

"You know her?" Maribel asked with wide eyes.

"Of course!" King Hollyberry placed a hand on his belly as he laughed. "Don't you?"

"No…." Maribel shook her head. "Should I?"

The fairy giggled. "You will now. And while I'm certain you can do this without my help, I cannot deny a wish." Fairy Princess Windgust curtsied with a smile. "I'm at your service and will offer any assistance you may need."

Maribel ruffled her feathers, set her withers, and said, "Let's stop that flood before the island is destroyed." She darted through the door, glancing over her shoulder. The fairy fluttered directly behind her. The other pegacorns and King Hollyberry also dashed through the door.

"There's no time to waste," Heidi said as they all traveled with great haste toward North Lake.

When they reached the lake, water was already seeping out onto the land. The ground absorbed the water like a sponge. Maribel stepped closer to the shore, the soil squishing beneath her hoof.

"This is terrible," Callie said as she lifted a mud-covered leg.

"It's worse," Noelle said. She pointed across the lake where small torrents raced downhill. But a large one, wider than a branch of Three Friends Stream, headed straight toward Autumnseve.

If Maribel didn't fix the problem quickly, the neighboring kingdom would be destroyed. She couldn't let that happen! "How can we possibly stop this?" Maribel asked Fairy Princess Windgust.

"It's *you* that must do the work. I'm only here to help." Windgust bowed. "Never fear, my friend. You have the power within you."

Maribel pawed at the ground with her hoof. "Yes, I do believe you're right." The problem was, Maribel didn't quite know how to stop the flood. "Let's go to the dam. Maybe we'll find a solution there."

"Good idea," Windgust said with a nod.

Maribel looked back and saw Heidi, Paisley, Callie, and King Hollyberry still standing at the edge of the lake. The king scratched his beard and the pegacorns each flapped their wings. They all appeared quite anxious about the overflowing lake.

But as Maribel crossed the bridge, she saw an even bigger problem ahead. "This is terrible."

"Much worse than I could have imagined." Windgust's eyes grew large with surprise.

The wall of the dam had large holes in it!

Water spurted out in giant streams. A rock tumbled out of place and fell to the ground.

"It's unstable. How will we ever repair this?" Maribel asked as she glimpsed down over the edge of the wall.

"It may not matter." Windgust looked frozen with fear as she shook her head. "The water levels are rising faster than ever."

"Then this could be the end of Avonlea as

we know it." Maribel pawed at the stone wall, and another piece crumbled. Water rushed through the new opening. "I can't allow such a thing to happen," she said, feeling a sudden surge of determination. She wouldn't let her beautiful island be destroyed. Maribel would fix the problem no matter what. "I have an idea!"

Fairy Princess Windgust turned abruptly toward the pegacorn. "You do?" She waved her wand in excitement. "What is it?"

"Well, I'm going to need your help." Maribel pawed her hoof with a chuff. "I can't do this alone."

"That's precisely why I'm here," Fairy Princess Windgust said. "You can count on me."

"Good." Maribel set her hooves and flapped her wings. "Are you able to plug the holes?"

Windgust pushed up her sleeves. "I can do that."

"And I'll stop the flood." Maribel lifted off the ground, her powerful wings helping her rise high into the sky.

Below, Fairy Princess Windgust gathered rocks. The fairy waved her wand. Glitter rained down and, as if on command, a stone squeezed into a hole. Maribel watched in awe, almost forgetting her own mission. One by one, Windgust sealed the leaks. "All set here!" she called out.

"Brilliant!" Maribel shouted down to the fairy. Windgust may have solved one problem, but Maribel still had work to do. Water levels rose rapidly, and Maribel worried the stone wall might burst. If it could withstand the pressure, then the water was sure to rise over the dam and flood the surrounding kingdoms. She needed to stop that from happening.

Beating her wings as hard as she could, Maribel felt the wind growing stronger. With each flap, the water at the top of the dam curled into little white-capped waves. But the flood was coming too fast. The water rushed forward, spilling over the edge of the dam, and a rock slipped. "Windgust! Hurry, the rocks are beginning to tumble."

Fluttering against the wind, the fairy waved her wand, sending sparkles to work their magic. Once the rocks were set in place, Windgust retreated to a treetop where the branches swayed wildly.

"Nice work!" Maribel flapped her wings harder, feeling stronger than she ever had before. *Come on wings, don't fail me now,* she thought. The water rolled into large whitecaps, rising higher and higher. Then the water did something Maribel never believed possible.

Chapter 16

The whitecaps folded in on themselves, making a massive splash! Then, like magic, they started rolling backwards.

"I can't believe it's really working!" Maribel shouted. "I never thought my wings could do that." She felt a sense of pride, knowing she could control the wind in ways she never realized before.

"Look at you!" Fairy Princess Windgust said as she fought against the breeze. "I knew you had it in you!"

"Thank you for believing in me," Maribel said with a neigh.

"Your strong wings give you the power to control the wind," Fairy Princess Windgust called out as gusts forced her from the branches. She fluttered steadily in the air as though she had been trained for this very moment. "Concentrate. Focus. It must obey your bidding."

Maribel closed her eyes and nodded. If her wings were powerful enough to change the direction of water, she wondered if it could do something else. Maribel wasn't certain how long she could hold the water at bay.

With her eyes still closed, Maribel directed the wind toward the water once again. *Focus,* she thought. *It might not work, but you won't know until you try.* Maribel opened her eyes and drew in a deep breath. She channeled the wind a different way, but the waters crept toward her.

"That's the wrong direction!" Windgust cried.

"Trust me," Maribel said. "I have an idea." She flapped her wings harder, focusing and calling on the wind to come from far away in the north. If she could draw in a cold front, she might just stop this flood.

Frosty air came from the mountains of Wintersend.

It came from beyond the Dragon Sea.

Maribel's strong wings drew in breezes that made the temperature drop. A chill blanketed the kingdom. She directed that cold air toward the water. As soon as it touched the surface of the lake, the water began to freeze.

"Whoa," Fairy Princess Windgust said with a gasp. "Brilliant work, my friend!"

Maribel chuffed. She tipped her head, her horn sparkling like ice. She sent another spiral of wind toward the dam. As the water flowed over the wall, it immediately froze into icicles.

"Over here!" Fairy Princess Windgust said, waving Maribel toward a stream. Water raced from the mountains of Wintersend. It swirled around trees and hollyberry bushes, making its way to Autumnseve.

Maribel flew toward the rushing water which threatened the neighboring kingdom. Hovering just above the ground, she beat her wings and created a current of freezing air. Maribel sent that wind straight toward the water. In an instant, it turned to ice.

"This way!" Fairy Princess Windgust flew off in the opposite direction, pointing to more streams which sprinted around the lake.

Water rushed past faster than the current in Rainbow River. And it was headed straight for the Purple Pumpkin Patch!

Chapter 17

*M*aribel flew toward the fairy. "There's more?"

"Yes, and you'll have to work fast," Fairy Princess Windgust said.

"I think I can do it." Maribel was tired but she needed to find her strength to save the pumpkins.

"You've already spared the island from ruin," Fairy Princess Windgust said. "I'm sure you can do this one last thing."

"You're right." Maribel nodded. She dug her hoof in and pawed at the ground with a chuff. "I can do this."

Flapping with all her might, Maribel stood on her hind legs. The river of melted snow raged downhill. Even the Rainbow River—with all its fast-flowing water—never moved nearly as quick.

"This flood will test my skill, strength, and endurance, but I won't allow it to win,"

Maribel said, flapping her magical wings. The wind whipped, but the water didn't listen and continued rushing onward. "You must stop!"

Fairy Princess Windgust bounced about in the air, fighting against the gusts as they threatened to send her spiraling into the next kingdom. "You can do it! Try a little harder."

Maribel flapped her wings again, urging the wind toward the river. The wind whipped and slapped the surface, but the water continued to rush downhill toward the Kingdom of Autumnseve.

"Hurry," Heidi said, galloping toward Maribel. "It's almost to the pumpkins!"

Paisley cantered up behind Heidi. "Please work quickly."

"I'm doing my best," Maribel neighed. "My wings are tired."

"Did you really do that?" King Hollyberry pointed to the frozen lake.

"I sure did," Maribel said as she beat her wings, pushing a large gust outward.

King Hollyberry braced himself against the wind. "Then you can do this, too."

"I'm tired," Maribel said.

"You must try," Heidi and Paisley said.

Callie and Noelle cheered, "We believe in you!"

"I'll do it." Maribel spread her wings and

willed the wind toward the flood water which raged like a river. Little white caps grew and soon curled in the opposite direction.

"That's it!" Paisley whinnied.

"You did it!" King Hollyberry said.

"You're something special," Callie called.

"You really are!" Noelle echoed from her perch on Callie's horn.

But then Maribel fell to the ground, exhausted. "It won't hold for long."

"Help her!" Heidi shouted. Her tail twitched. She turned to scold it but then shook her head. "This won't end well."

Paisley and King Hollyberry helped Maribel to her hooves.

Maribel felt weak and wobbled in place. She was much too tired. "I can't do it."

"You have to try," Fairy Princess Windgust said.

Maribel took a deep breath, longing to find hidden strength but it felt impossible. Her energy was zapped. She tried flapping her wings, but they ached, and she couldn't lift them.

"Don't give up." Fairy Princess Windgust flew to Maribel's side. "You're the pegacorn of wind. Think about your magic. You have special powers. Do you really believe it's just in your wings?"

"But it's my wings that do all the work," Maribel said.

Fairy Princess Windgust stroked Maribel's icy blue mane. "Are you certain?"

"I don't know." Maribel shook her head. "It's all I've ever used before. My wings have never failed me."

"Then it's time you consider where your magic really comes from," Fairy Princess Windgust said, patting the pegacorn's head.

Could Fairy Princess Windgust be right? Maybe that's what Grandfather Merlin had meant, too, Maribel thought. *It wasn't just her wings that controlled the wind. Maybe the magic came from somewhere else entirely.*

"I guess it wouldn't hurt to try." Maribel closed her eyes. Instead of using her wings, Maribel simply imagined drawing cold air from Mount Wintersend.

She imagined bringing chilly breezes from beyond Dragon Sea.

She imagined the water obeying her command.

She imagined her magic.

Maribel didn't just have powerful wings, she had powerful *magic*. For the first time, she *felt* it. Really felt it. In her horn, in her hooves. And most importantly, in her heart.

"Whoa!" Heidi gasped. "Look!"

When Maribel opened her eyes, she saw large clumps of ice floating along the river. The things she had imagined had truly happened! "I did that?"

"You did it without even using your wings, Maribel!" Paisley shook her mane as she reared back with a loud whinny.

"I knew you had it in you," Fairy Princess Windgust said. "Now do you believe me?"

"I sure do. And I have another idea." Maribel thought if her magic could control the wind, then her strong wings were a driving force. "It's time to finish the job. Watch this!" Maribel focused, summoning strength from deep within and flapped her wings. Using all her might, she channeled the breeze into a colossal wind which whirled in a circle.

"Be careful," King Hollyberry said, pulling his cloak around him as he turned his back to the wind. "We don't need a tornado."

"*S*he can control it," Paisley said as she flapped her wings to steady herself. "Can't you, Maribel?"

"Certainly." Maribel beat her wings again and, with a nod of her head, the tunnel turned into an enormous cyclone. As the cyclone touched the water's surface, Maribel folded her wings against her body. She breathed steadily and focused. The twister spun to a stop and the wind within it slowly crept out like a misty fog. The river crackled, freezing instantly.

Heidi inspected the ice and then turned to Maribel. "You've really done it!" The friends rubbed shoulders.

"You're truly magical," Paisley said as she joined the two pegacorns.

"You've saved the pumpkins," a mighty voice said. "And you found your magic."

Maribel gasped. "Yes, I did, Grandfather Merlin. I *really* did."

"On behalf of the dragons, we wish to thank you." Grandfather Merlin stepped back and watched with an approving nod.

Callie trotted over. "Thank you, my dear friend for freezing the flood. You've saved the kingdom!"

"It's a relief that you're feeling better," Maribel said, nuzzling up against Callie.

"You're a hero!" Noelle chirped as she twittered above Callie's horn.

"Thank you," Maribel blushed and tipped her head toward the ground, which had once been entirely covered by snow. Blades of grass poked out of the soil. It was strange to see the kingdom like this, but she was relieved to know she'd diverted a disaster.

The four pegacorn friends huddled together. They spread their wings and wrapped each other in a giant hug.

"My work here is done," Fairy Princess Windgust said.

Maribel reared up. "I couldn't have done it without you!"

"You did the hard part. I only helped you find your magic." Windgust fluttered her wings and flew off into the distance. Soon she disappeared completely from sight.

"Excellent work, my pegacorn friends," King Hollyberry said, marching up to the group.

Maribel winked at Callie, and together they pulled the king into the hug with their wings. The friends whinnied and neighed.

"I told you it would be fine!" Heidi said to her tail.

Paisley giggled.

Heidi scowled and flicked her tail, snapping it against Paisley's hindquarters. Then they smiled at each other and laughed. "Let's hear it for Maribel," they said.

Everyone cheered for the pegacorn of wind.

"You saved the day!" Callie exclaimed.

Maribel bowed her head. This day had taught her so much. She discovered she had the magic to save her kingdom. She finally understood her power. Most of all, she learned that with a little bit of magic, a lot of strength, and some teamwork, she could accomplish anything.

"Maribel did more than that," Paisley said. "She saved Avonlea!"

Spreading her mighty wings and flapping them with all her strength, Maribel whinnied. She smiled and said, "We all did."

More magic awaits!

When Fiona's shell goes missing, she must find it before her gift of song is also lost at sea.

Turn the page for a peek at the next book in the Unicorn Tales series!

Fiona's Missing Shell

It was a beautiful morning in the Kingdom of Springsmorn and Fiona, a teal-colored unicorn, stood at the bank of Rainbow River. Fluffy white clouds rolled across a bright blue sky. The sun's rays sparkled and danced on the colorful water. Fiona gazed into the current, watching the fish swim past and saw her reflection gazing back. The image of her wavy green mane rippled in the rush of the water, looking so much like waterweed a few fish hesitated before swimming past.

"Where are you going?" Fiona asked the fish. They always seemed to be in such a hurry as they rushed downstream. In fact, they only seemed to go in one direction. Always downstream. "And why don't you ever go back from where you've come?"

A fish bobbed its rainbow-colored head out of the water. "We go to South Lake," the fish said. "The water is fine and there's lots of food."

Fiona normally only traveled to South Lake for Elle's birthday celebration. Her yearly visits were enough to remind her of the lake's beauty. It was a beautiful body of water that stretched across the southern part of the Kingdom of Summerstart. While Fiona loved lazing about by the banks of Blossom Lagoon, she often dreamt of enjoying sunny lakeside days at the glorious water in the southern kingdom.

"That sounds lovely," Fiona said to the fish. "I should like to go there, too, but this is my kingdom and I'm needed here."

"I know," the fish said.

Fiona blinked. She didn't realize the fish knew so much about the unicorns. "You do?"

"Absolutely," the fish said with a glug, glug, glug. "I also know that your name is Fiona."

"That's right," the unicorn said, rearing back on her hind hooves.

The fish leapt out of the water, flipping its tail mid-air. "I'm here to deliver a special gift just for you."

"A gift for me?" Fiona briefly believed she

was dreaming. No one had ever given her a gift before. Especially not a fish. "Who is it from?"

"Someone special," the fish said.

"But who would want to bring me a gift?" Fiona asked.

"No time for questions," the fish said with a wave of its fin.

Fiona thought for a moment. She needed answers. "But…"

"Don't worry and never fear," the fish said. "The gift is from me."

Fiona shook her head. "But why should you want to give me a gift?"

"Because you're the one who has been chosen." The fish dipped its head back into the water and bubbles rose to the surface.

"Chosen? For what?" Fiona bent closer to the water to inspect the fish. She tipped her head, observing her reflection that seemed to hide the fish from view.

The fish poked his head out of the water again. "For a special purpose."

"What is it then?" Fiona neighed with delight. She *felt* special. Truth be told, she'd always known she was special but now someone else knew it, too.

"Patience!" the fish said. "You'll see." The fish flipped its tail and a small shell bounced off of its fin.

A white shell tumbled across the pebble-lined bank and came to a rolling stop just in front of Fiona's hoof.

"What a beautiful shell!" Fiona said as she admired the fan-like shape. The inside of the shell glowed with a hidden rainbow.

"It's not just any shell," the fish said as it swam closer to shore.

Fiona squinted as she inspected the delicate gift. "It's not?"

"Of course not. It's a *magic* shell." The fish bobbed its head out of the water, one eye staring straight at the unicorn.

"Magic?" Fiona oohed with delight. She loved magic. In fact, Fiona had her very own special gift of music which she shared with the other unicorns in her kingdom. While she never quite considered it magical, the other unicorns assured Fiona that her gift was quite special. She'd always longed to find her song, however, but she struggled to discover the right tune.

"Yes," the fish said with a flip of its tail.

Fiona was unsure of how a shell could be magical, but she wanted to believe the fish. "What kind of magic?"

"The magic of knowledge." The fish fought the current, swimming in place.

"Oh, I see," Fiona said, nudging the shell with her hoof.

"You've been chosen as the guardian," the fish said. "You will need to keep it safe and protected from anyone who would seek to do harm. Some would use the knowledge for the wrong things."

Fiona nodded with wide eyes. While all of the unicorns on Avonlea were kind and worked together, she knew those pixies were quite mischievous. They'd been known to cause a great deal of problems. While she'd never been to Dragonfire Forest, she wasn't sure if the dragons could be trusted either.

"You have my word," Fiona said with a neigh. "I will keep it safe."

The fish glugged in the water, bubbles rising to the surface. He made a big splash as he then leapt out of the water once again. "There's just one more thing you should know."

"What's that?" Fiona asked the fish.

"If you lose it," the fish said as he puckered his lips, "you'll also lose your song."

A NOTE FROM THE AUTHOR

Thank you, dear reader, for returning to read another Unicorn Tales adventure! I'm so grateful and honored to bring them to you.

Maribel's Windy Rescue was another story that was a long time in the making. This book was first plotted, outlined, and summarized in 2019. Then I let the story stew while I worked on other books. When I returned to read the first draft, I realized three of the most important plot markers just simply weren't working. The story required a major overhaul.

This began to weigh on me as I realized rewrites were becoming a pattern. I started to question myself. What if I couldn't craft another story? What if my readers disliked my books? These questions made me doubt myself. Like my unicorns, sometimes I, too, struggle with confidence.

But then I'd receive a note or words of encouragement from a parent or reader and it brightened my day. It helped me find the courage to keep trying. I knew you and other readers were waiting for these stories and I didn't want to disappoint any of you!

I can't thank you enough for trusting me to bring you more books. It is my great pleasure to write these stories and share the unicorns of Avonlea with you. There is so much more to come - lots of exciting things in the works - and I can't wait to share them with you!

If you enjoyed this story, please tell your friends, parents, grandparents, guardians, teachers, and anyone who loves books! Reviews are so appreciated as they help me find new readers, and help readers find great books.

Thanks again for your support!

Stay magical,

— AMIE BORST

ABOUT THE AUTHOR

Amie Borst is a multi-award winning author of several books for children including the Scarily Every Laughter series (Cinderskella, Little Dead Riding Hood, Snow Fright), the Doomy Prepper series, and Unicorn Tales! Amie believes in unicorns, loves glitter, and keeps a stash of chocolate hidden away from her chocolate-stealing family.

Want to keep up with the latest releases and be the first to learn about new projects? Visit Amie's website for more information. While you're there, be sure to have a parent or guardian sign up for her newsletter so you can receive updates on new books, sales, and promotions.

Website: www.amieborst.com

facebook.com/amieborstauthor

instagram.com/amieborst

ABOUT THE ILLUSTRATOR

Roch Hercka is an artist, illustrator, painter, and book lover. This is his second children's book series, having previously illustrated the Scarily Ever Laughter series. Roch enjoys painting, reading comic books, playing board games, and watching movies. He lives in Torun, Poland with his family and a cat. Visit his websites to see more of his beautiful creations!

Illustrations: www.hercka.carbonmade.com

Paintings: www.roch.carbonmade.com

facebook.com/RochHerckaArt

instagram.com/Rochart_85

FOLLOW UNICORN TALES

Learn all the latest and exciting updates on Unicorn Tales!

Want to keep up with the latest information about this magical series? Be sure to follow Unicorn Tales on Instagram and Facebook for fun book information, reels, and updates including book releases and new products!

 facebook.com/UnicornTalesSeries
instagram.com/Unicorn_Tales_Series

Made in the USA
Middletown, DE
08 February 2022